Kitty
Goes to School

by Jerry Smath

Cartwheel
·B·O·O·K·S·®

SCHOLASTIC INC.
New York   Toronto   London   Auckland   Sydney
Mexico City   New Delhi   Hong Kong   Buenos Aires

"Wake up, Kitty," says Mother.
"Wake up, sleepyhead," says Father.
"You don't want to be late
for your first day of school."

After breakfast,
Kitty is ready for school.
Mother lets her
wear a new hat.

Kitty is still a little sleepy.
She gets dressed
and brushes her hair.

Kitty waits for the school bus to come.
"Where are the other kids?" she asks.
"None of the other children on our street
are big enough to go to school,"
says Mother.

The bus is already full of kids.
Kitty feels all grown-up
as she waves good-bye
to her mother.

Kitty gives her mother a kiss
and gets on the school bus.
"Nice hat!" says the driver.

The school bus stops in front of the school.
A nice lady is waiting to meet the kids.
"Hello," she says. "I am your teacher.
My name is Ms. Hopper."
Ms. Hopper takes Kitty and the other children
to their classroom.

Kitty loves
her new classroom.
It is filled
with really neat things.

"This is where we will learn and have fun," says Ms. Hopper. Then she opens the door.

After the children get to know each other, Ms. Hopper starts class for the day. "Let's make pretty pictures to hang in the window," she says.

Kitty draws a picture of herself.
"Very good!" says Ms. Hopper.
"I will hang it
with the others."

All the kids start to draw
their pictures.
Ms. Hopper puts up a string
to hang them on.

"Now we will start to learn our letters,"
says Ms. Hopper.
"Pick a letter from this pile," she tells her class.
Everyone picks a letter — even Ms. Hopper.

Pup picks A for Apple.
Kitty picks M for Mouse.
And Ms. Hopper picks U for Umbrella.

Some of the children
do not know their letters.
"Don't worry," says Ms. Hopper.
"I am here to help you learn them.
Now let's find your letters
in the alphabet."

It is fun learning letters,
but now it is time to play.
Ms. Hopper blows *toot-toot* on a little horn.
Kitty and the other kids
follow her outside to the playground.

Ms. Hopper joins in the fun.
"Hold on tight," Kitty tells her.

Some of the kids like the slide.
Kitty likes to jump rope
best of all.

Back in the classroom it is story time.
Today is Kitty's day to pick a book.
"Quiet, class," says Ms. Hopper.
"I know you will like the story
that Kitty has picked."

The story is really good.
Soon everyone forgets
that they are in a classroom.
Kitty feels just like the princess
who lives in the sea.

Everyone is quiet
as Ms. Hopper reads.
The story is about a princess
who lives in the sea.

Just as Ms. Hopper is done reading,
there is a knock on the door.
It is a father and his little daughter.
"I'm sorry my daughter is so late
for class," he tells Ms. Hopper.

"Tina will be fine,"
Ms. Hopper tells him.
"Class is almost over.
But she can stay with us
until it's time to go."

"This is my little girl, Tina,"
says the father.
"We have just moved here.
Tina missed the bus
and now she doesn't want
to go to school."

Everyone makes Tina feel right at home.
"Why don't you show Tina her new classroom?"
Ms. Hopper asks Kitty.
Tina likes her teacher and her new friends —
especially Kitty!

When Kitty comes back,
they both start to laugh.
"See!" says Kitty.
"We have the same hat."

"School is over for today!"
Ms. Hopper tells the class.
Kitty goes to get her things.
"I have something to show you,"
she tells Tina.

It has been a good day for Kitty
and her friends.
Ms. Hopper makes sure that
everyone gets on the bus.
"See you tomorrow," she calls as the
school bus takes the children home.

Now Kitty and Tina
are the only kids on the bus.
"We must live on the same street!"
says Kitty.

One by one, the kids
get off the bus.
"Last stop coming up,"
says the driver.

Kitty's mother and Tina's father
are waiting for them.
"How was your first day of school?"
asks Kitty's mother.
"It was really neat," says Kitty,
"and I have a new friend, too!"

And when they play school,
they take turns playing teacher.

Now Kitty and Tina
play together
almost every day.

To Oladine Parker, wherever you are.
-J.S.

Copyright © 2003 by Jerry Smath. All rights reserved. Published by Scholastic Inc.

ISBN 0-439-44611-2

10 9 8 7 6 5 4 3 2 1   03 04 05 06 07

Printed in the U.S.A. 08 • First printing, July 2003